For Amanda Hodge Redd, my beloved mommy.
Thank you for being my best friend and my ultimate role model. —N.R.

For Mama. We love you dearly. —N.M.

Text copyright © 2020 by Nancy Redd
Jacket art and interior illustrations copyright © 2020 by Nneka Myers

Visit us on the Web! rhcbooks.com

Educators and librarians, for a variety of teaching tools, visit us at RHTeachersLibrarians.com

Library of Congress Cataloging-in-Publication Data
Names: Redd, Nancy Amanda, author. | Myers, Nneka, illustrator.
Title: Bedtime bonnet / Nancy Redd; illustrated by Nneka Myers.
Description: New York: Random House, [2020] | Summary: As family members braid, brush, twirl, roll,
and tighten their hair before bedtime, putting on kerchiefs, wave caps, and other protective items, the little sister cannot find her bonnet.
Identifiers: LCCN 2019020431 | ISBN 978-1-9848-9524-0 (hardcover) | ISBN 978-1-9848-9525-7 (lib. bdg.) | ISBN 978-1-9848-9526-4 (ebook)
Subjects: | CYAC: Hair—Fiction. | Headgear—Fiction. | Family life—Fiction. | African Americans—Fiction. | Bedtime—Fiction.
Classification: LCC PZ7.1.R3995 Bed 2020 | DDC [E]—dc23

MANUFACTURED IN CHINA
10 9 8 7 6 5 4 3 2 1
First Edition

Bedtime Bonnet

By Nancy Redd

Illustrated by Nneka Myers

Random House 🏠 New York

In my family, when the sun goes down, our hair goes up!

My brother twists and tightens each of his locs.

Sis combs her hair in a swirl round her head.

Daddy's hairbrush makes rows of black waves appear.

Grandma rolls up her silver mane.

Grandpa doesn't do anything to his hair—because he doesn't have any!

After Mommy gathers her corkscrew curls in a scarf, she calls for me.
I scoot between her legs, and she gets to work on my hair.
I'm tenderheaded, so she's extra gentle.

Grandpa tells jokes as Mommy works her magic.
He asks me, "Why does the bee have sticky hair?"
I don't know, so he says, "Because it uses a honeycomb!"
Silly Grandpa!

Finally, a braided crown is on top of my head, and it's time for bed.

Except . . .

I can't find my bedtime bonnet!

I need it to protect my hair from tangles and lint while I sleep.

Wearing my bonnet at night is as important as brushing my teeth!

Maybe Grandma knows where it is. She's covering her rollers with a kerchief. "Grandma, have you seen my bonnet?"

She gets up and looks around.
"No, dear, I haven't. Maybe your
sister knows?"

My sister's still in the bathroom, her hair spun in a wrap.
"Sis, have you seen my bonnet?"

She looks in all the bathroom drawers.
"No, but here's Daddy's wave cap."

I take the cap to Daddy, and he pops it onto his waves.
"Daddy, have you seen my bonnet?"

He looks around the sofa, but it's not there, either.

I can't go to bed without it!

Just then, my big brother walks in, a durag slipped over his locs.

Does he know where it is?

"Big bro, have you seen my bonnet?"

He doesn't even pretend to look. He just says, "Ask Grandpa!"

Oh, Grandpa!

My bonnet is now in its proper place, and I'm really sleepy.
Everyone gives me kisses and hugs, and Mommy and Daddy read me a story.
Good night, family!

In the morning, when the sun comes up, our hair comes down!

Daddy smooths his ocean-like waves.
Mommy scrunches her ribbony curls.

Sis unwinds her foot-long wrap.
My brother shakes out his lovely locs.

While Grandma unsnaps her rollers,
Grandpa shaves his head.

And as for me, my bonnet comes off and my braids come out.

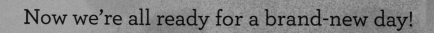

Now we're all ready for a brand-new day!